A Voyage
to Lilliput

JONATHAN SWIFT

A Phoenix Paperback

Gulliver's Travels first published in Everyman's Library in 1906.
Reissued 1991.

This abridged edition contains Chapters I to V of 'A Voyage to Lilliput'
and was first published in Great Britain in 1996 by Phoenix,
a Division of Orion Books Ltd,
Orion House, 5 Upper St Martin's Lane, London WC2H 9EA

ISBN 1 85799 621 6

Typeset by CentraCet Ltd, Cambridge
Printed in Great Britain by
Clays Ltd, St Ives plc

CHAPTER I

The author giveth some account of himself and family; his first inducements to travel. He is shipwrecked, and swims for his life; gets safe on shore in the country of Lilliput; is made a prisoner, and carried up the country.

My father had a small estate in Nottinghamshire; I was the third of five sons. He sent me to Emanuel-College in Cambridge, at fourteen years old, where I resided three years, and applied my self close to my studies: but the charge of maintaining me (although I had a very scanty allowance) being too great for a narrow fortune; I was bound apprentice to Mr James Bates, an eminent surgeon in London, with whom I continued four years; and my father now and then sending me small sums of money, I laid them out in learning navigation, and other parts of the mathematicks, useful to those who intend to travel, as I always believed it would be some time or other my fortune to do. When I left Mr Bates, I went down to my father, where, by the assistance of him and my Uncle John, and some other relations, I got forty pounds, and a promise of thirty pounds a year to maintain me at Leyden: there I studied physick two years and seven months, knowing it would be useful in long voyages.

Soon after my return from Leyden, I was recommended by my good master Mr Bates, to be surgeon to the *Swallow*, Captain Abraham Pannell commander; with whom I continued three years and a half, making a voyage or two into the Levant, and some other parts. When I came back, I resolved to settle in London, to which Mr Bates, my master, encouraged me; and by him I was recommended to several patients. I took part of a small house in the Old-Jury; and being advised to alter my condition, I married Mrs Mary Burton, second daughter to Mr Edmond Burton, hosier, in Newgate-street, with whom I received four hundred pounds for a portion.

But, my good master Bates dying in two years after, and I having few friends, my business began to fail; for my conscience would not suffer me to imitate the bad practice of too many among my brethren. Having therefore consulted with my wife, and some of my acquaintance, I determined to go again to sea. I was surgeon successively in two ships, and made several voyages, for six years, to the East and West-Indies; by which I got some addition to my fortune. My hours of leisure I spent in reading the best authors, ancient and modern; being always provided with a good number of books; and when I was ashore, in observing the manners and dispositions of the people, as well as learning their language; wherein I had a great facility by the strength of my memory.

The last of these voyages not proving very fortunate, I grew weary of the sea, and intended to stay at home with my wife and family. I removed from the Old-Jury to Fetter-lane, and from thence to Wapping, hoping to get business among the sailors; but it would not turn to account. After three years expectation, that things would mend, I accepted an advantageous offer from Captain William Prichard, master of the *Antelope*, who was making a voyage to the South-Sea. We set sail from Bristol, May 4th, 1699, and our voyage at first was very prosperous.

It would not be proper for some reasons, to trouble the reader with the particulars of our adventures in those seas: let it suffice to inform him, that in our passage from thence to the East-Indies, we were driven by a violent storm to the north-west of Van Diemen's Land. By an observation, we found ourselves in the latitude of 30 degrees 2 minutes south. Twelve of our crew were dead by immoderate labour, and ill food; the rest were in a very weak condition. On the fifth of

November, which was the beginning of summer in those parts, the weather being very hazy, the seamen spyed a rock, within half a cable's length of the ship; but the wind was so strong, that we were driven directly upon it, and immediately split. Six of the crew, of whom I was one, having let down the boat into the sea, made a shift to get clear of the ship, and the rock. We rowed by my computation, about three leagues, until we were able to work no longer, being already spent with labour while we were in the ship: we therefore trusted ourselves to the mercy of the waves; and in about half an hour the boat was overset by a sudden flurry from the north. What became of my companions in the boat, as well as of those who escaped on the rock, or were left in the vessel, I cannot tell; but conclude they were all lost. For my own part, I swam as fortune directed me, and was pushed forward by wind and tide. I often let my legs drop; and could feel no bottom: but when I was almost gone, and able to struggle no longer, I found myself within my depth; and by this time the storm was much abated. The declivity was so small, that I walked near a mile before I got to the shore, which I conjectured was about eight o'clock in the evening. I then advanced forward near half a mile, but could not discover any sign of houses or inhabitants; at least I was in so weak a condition, that I did not observe them. I was extremely tired, and with that, and the heat of the weather, and about half a pint of brandy that I drank as I left the ship, I found myself much inclined to sleep. I lay down on the grass, which was very short and soft; where I slept sounder than ever I remember to have done in my life, and as I reckoned, above nine hours; for when I awaked, it was just day-light. I attempted to rise, but was not able to stir: for, as I happened to lie on my back, I found my arms and legs were strongly fastned on each side to the ground; and my hair, which was long and thick, tied down in the same manner. I likewise felt several slender ligatures across my body, from my arm-pits to my thighs. I could only look upwards; the sun began to grew hot, and the light offended mine eyes. I heard a confused noise about me, but in the posture I lay, could see nothing except the sky. In a little time I felt something alive moving on my left leg, which advancing gently forward over my breast, came almost up to my chin; when bending mine eyes downwards as much as I could, I perceived it to be a human creature not six inches high, with a bow and arrow in his hands, and a quiver at his back. In the mean time, I felt at least forty more of the same kind (as I conjectured) following the first. I was in the utmost astonishment, and 5 roared so loud, that they all run back in a fright; and some of them, as I was afterwards told, were hurt with the falls they got by leaping from my sides upon the ground. However, they soon returned; and one of them, who ventured so far as to get a full sight of my face, lifting up his hands and eyes by way of admiration, cryed out in a shrill, but distinct voice, 'Hekina degul': the others repeated the same words several times, but I then knew not what they meant. I lay all this while, as the reader may believe, in great uneasiness: at length, struggling to get loose, I had the fortune to break the strings, and wrench out the pegs that fastned my left arm to the ground: for, by lifting it up to my face, I discovered the methods they had taken to bind me; and, at the same time, with a violent pull, which gave me excessive pain, I a little loosened the strings that tied down my hair on the left side; so that I was just able to turn my head about two inches. But the creatures ran off a second time, before I could seize them; whereupon there was a great shout in a very shrill accent; and after it ceased, I heard one of them cry aloud, 'Tolgo Phonac'; when in an instant, I felt above an hundred arrows discharged on my left hand, which pricked me like so many needles; and besides, they shot another flight into the air, as we do bombs in Europe; whereof many, I suppose, fed on my body, (though I felt them not) and some on my face, which I immediately covered with my left hand. When this shower of arrows was over, I fell a groaning with grief and pain; and then striving again to get loose, they discharged another volley larger than the first; and some of them attempted with spears to stick me in the sides; but, by good luck, I had on me a buff jerkin, which they could not pierce. I thought it the most prudent method to lie still; and my design was to continue so until night, when my left hand being already loose, I could easily free my self: and, as for the inhabitants, I had reason to believe I might be a match for the greatest armies they could bring against me, if they were all of the same size with him that I saw. But fortune disposed otherwise of me. When the people observed I was quiet, they discharged no more arrows: but by the noise encreasing, I knew their numbers were greater; and about four yards from me over against my right ear, I heard a knocking for above an hour, like people at work; when turning my head that way, as well as the pegs and strings would permit me, I saw a stage erected about a foot and a half from the ground, capable of holding four of the inhabitants, with two or three ladders to mount it: from whence one of them, who seemed to be a person of quality, made me a long speech, whereof I understood not one 7

syllable. But I should have mentioned, that before the principal person began his oration, he cryed out three times 'Langro dehul san': (these words and the former were afterwards repeated and explained to me.) Whereupon immediately about fifty of the inhabitants came, and cut the strings that fastened the left side of my head, which gave me the liberty of turning it to the right, and of observing the person and gesture of him who was to speak. He appeared to be of a middle age, and taller than any of the other three who attended him; whereof one was a page, who held up his train, and seemed to be somewhat longer than my middle finger; the other two stood one on each side to support him. He acted every part of an orator; and I could observe many periods of threatnings, and others of promises, pity, and kindness. I answered in a few words, but in the most submissive manner, lifting up my left hand and both mine eyes to the sun, as calling him for a witness; and being almost famished with hunger, having not eaten a morsel for some hours before I left the ship, I found the demands of nature so strong upon me, that I could not forbear shewing my impatience (perhaps against the strict rules of decency) by putting my finger frequently on my mouth, to signify that I wanted food. The Hurgo (for so they call
8 a great lord, as I afterwards learnt) understood me

very well: he descended from the stage, and commanded that several ladders should be applied to my sides, on which above an hundred of the inhabitants mounted and walked towards my mouth, laden with baskets full of meat, which had been provided, and sent thither by the king's orders upon the first intelligence he received of me. I observed there was the flesh of several animals, but could not distinguish them by the taste. There were shoulders, legs, and loins shaped like those of mutton, and very well dressed, but smaller than the wings of a lark. I eat them by two or three at a mouthful; and took three loaves at a time, about the bigness of musket-bullets. They supplyed me as fast as they could, shewing a thousand marks of wonder and astonishment at my bulk and appetite. I then made another sign that I wanted drink. They found by my eating that a small quantity would not suffice me; and being a most ingenious people, they slung up with great dexterity one of their largest hogsheads; then rolled it towards my hand, and beat out the top; I drank it off at a draught, which I might well do, for it hardly held half a pint, and tasted like a small wine of Burgundy, but much more delicious. They brought me a second hogshead, which I drank in the same manner, and made signs for more, but they had none to give me. When I had performed these wonders, they 9

shouted for joy, and danced upon my breast, repeating several times as they did at first, 'Hekinah degul.' They made me a sign, that I should throw down the two hogsheads, but first warned the people below to stand out of the way, crying aloud, 'Borach mivola'; and when they saw the vessels in the air, there was an universal shout of 'Hekinah degul.' I confess I was often tempted, while they were passing backwards and forwards on my body, to seize forty or fifty of the first that came in my reach, and dash them against the ground. But the remembrance of what I had felt, which probably might not be the worst they could do; and the promise of honour I made them, for so I interpreted my submissive behaviour, soon drove out those imaginations. Besides, I now considered my self as bound by the laws of hospitality to a people who had treated me with so much expence and magnificence. However, in my thoughts I could not sufficiently wonder at the intrepidity of these diminutive mortals, who durst venture to mount and walk on my body, while one of my hands was at liberty, without trembling at the very sight of so prodigious a creature as I must appear to them. After some time, when they observed, that I made no more demands for meat, there appeared before me a person of high rank from
10 his Imperial Majesty. His excellency having mounted

on the small of my right leg, advanced forwards up to my face, with about a dozen of his retinue; and producing his credentials under the signet royal, which he applied close to mine eyes, spoke about ten minutes, without any signs of anger, but with a kind of determinate resolution; often pointing forwards, which, as I afterwards found was towards the capital city, about half a mile distant, whither it was agreed by his Majesty in council that I must be conveyed. I answered in few words, but to no purpose, and made a sign with my hand that was loose, putting it to the other, (but over his excellency's head, for fear of hurting him or his train) and then to my own head and body, to signify that I desired my liberty. It appeared that he understood me well enough; for he shook his head by way of disapprobation, and held his hand in a posture to shew that I must be carried as a prisoner. However, he made other signs to let me understand, that I should have meat and drink enough, and very good treatment. Whereupon I once more thought of attempting to break my bonds; but again, when I felt the smart of their arrows upon my face and hands, which were all in blisters, and many of the darts still sticking in them; and observing likewise, that the number of my enemies encreased; I gave tokens to let them know that they might do with me what they pleased. Upon this, the

Hurgo and his train withdrew, with much civility and cheerful countenances. Soon after I heard a general shout, with frequent repetitions of the words, 'Peplom selan,' and I felt great numbers of the people on my left side relaxing the cords to such a degree, that I was able to turn upon my right, and to ease my self with making water; which I very plentifully did, to the great astonishment of the people, who conjecturing by my motions what I was going to do, immediately opened to the right and left on that side, to avoid the torrent which fell with such noise and violence from me. But before this, they had dawbed my face and both my hands with a sort of ointment very pleasant to the smell, which in a few minutes removed all the smart of their arrows. These circumstances, added to the refreshment I had received by their victuals and drink, which were very nourishing, disposed me to sleep. I slept about eight hours as I was afterwards assured; and it was no wonder; for the physicians, by the emperor's order had mingled a sleeping potion in the hogsheads of wine.

It seems, that upon the first moment I was discovered sleeping on the ground after my landing, the emperor had early notice of it by an express; and determined in council, that I should be tyed in the manner I have related; (which was done in the night while I slept) that plenty of meat and drink should be sent me, and a machine prepared to carry me to the capital city.

This resolution perhaps may appear very bold and dangerous, and I am confident would not be imitated by any prince in Europe on the like occasion; however, in my opinion, it was extremely prudent as well as generous. For, supposing these people had endeavoured to kill me with their spears and arrows while I was asleep; I should certainly have awaked with the first sense of smart, which might so far have rouzed my rage and strength, as to enable me to break the strings wherewith I was tyed; after which, as they were not able to make resistance, so they could expect no mercy.

These people are most excellent mathematicians, and arrived to a great perfection in mechanicks, by the countenance and encouragement of the emperor, who is a renowned patron of learning. This prince hath several machines fixed on wheels, for the carriage of trees and other great weights. He often buildeth his largest men of war, whereof some are nine foot long, in the woods where the timber grows, and has them carried on these engines three or four hundred yards to the sea. Five hundred carpenters and engineers were immediately set at work to prepare the greatest engine they had. It was a frame of wood raised three inches from the ground, about seven foot long and four wide, moving upon twenty two wheels. The shout I heard, was upon the arrival of this engine, which, it seems, set out in four hours after my landing. It was brought parallel to me as I lay. But the principal difficulty was to raise and place me in this vehicle. Eighty poles, each of one foot high, were erected for this purpose, and very strong cords of the bigness of packthread were fastened by hooks to many bandages, which the workmen had girt round my neck, my hands, my body, and my legs. Nine hundred of the strongest men were employed to draw up these cords by many pullies fastened on the poles; and thus in less than three hours, I was raised and slung into the engine, and there tyed fast. All this I was told; for while the whole operation was performing, I lay in a profound sleep, by the force of that soporiferous medicine infused into my liquor. Fifteen hundred of the emperor's largest horses, each about four inches and a half high, were employed to draw me towards the metropolis, which, as I said, was half a mile distant.

About four hours after we began our journey, I awaked by a very ridiculous accident; for the carriage being stopt a while to adjust something that was out of order, two or three of the young natives had the curiosity to see how I looked when I was asleep; they climbed up into the engine, and advancing very softly to my face, one of them, an officer in the guards, put the sharp end of his half-pike a good way up into my left nostril, which tickled my nose like a straw, and made me sneeze violently: whereupon they stole off unperceived; and it was three weeks before I knew the cause of my awaking so suddenly. We made a long march the remaining part of the day, and rested at night with five hundred guards on each side of me, half with torches, and half with bows and arrows, ready to shoot me if I should offer to stir. The next morning at sunrise we continued our march, and arrived within two hundred yards of the city-gates about noon. The emperor, and all his court, came out to meet us; but his great officers would by no means suffer his Majesty to endanger his person by mounting on my body.

At the place where the carriage stopt, there stood an ancient temple, esteemed to be the largest in the whole kingdom; which having been polluted some years before by an unnatural murder, was, according to the zeal of those people, looked upon as prophane, and therefore had been applied to common use, and all the ornaments and furniture carried away. In this edifice it was determined I should lodge. The great gate fronting to the north was about four feet high, and almost two feet wide, through which I could easily creep. On each side of the gate was a small window not above six inches from the ground: into that on the left side, the king's smiths conveyed fourscore and eleven chains, like those that hang to a lady's watch in Europe, and almost as large, which were locked to my left leg with six and thirty padlocks. Over against this temple, on the other side of the great highway, at twenty feet distance, there was a turret at least five feet high. Here the emperor ascended with many principal lords of his court, to have an opportunity of viewing me, as I was told, for I could not see them. It was reckoned that above an hundred thousand inhabitants came out of the town upon the same errand; and in spight of my guards, I believe there could not be fewer than ten thousand, at several times, who mounted upon my body by the help of ladders. But a proclamation was soon issued to forbid it, upon pain of death. When the workmen found it was impossible for me to break loose, they cut all the strings that bound me; whereupon I rose up with as melancholly a disposition as ever I had in my life. But the noise and astonishment of the people at seeing me rise and walk, are not to be expressed. The chains that held my left leg were about

two yards long, and gave me not only the liberty of

walking backwards and forwards in a semi-circle; but being fixed within four inches of the gate, allowed me to creep in, and lie at my full length in the temple.

CHAPTER II

The Emperor of Lilliput, attended by several of the nobility, comes to see the author in his confinement. The emperor's person and habit described. Learned men appointed to teach the author their language. He gains favour by his mild disposition. His pockets are searched, and his sword and pistols taken from him.

When I found my self on my feet, I looked about me, and must confess I never beheld a more entertaining prospect. The country round appeared like a continued garden; and the inclosed fields, which were generally forty feet square, resembled so many beds of flowers. These fields were intermingled with woods of half a stang, and the tallest trees, as I could judge, appeared to be seven feet high. I viewed the town on my left hand, which looked like the painted scene of a city in a theatre.

I had been for some hours extremely pressed by the

necessities of nature; which was no wonder, it being almost two days since I had last disburthened my self. I was under great difficulties between urgency and shame. The best expedient I could think on, was to creep into my house, which I accordingly did; and shutting the gate after me, I went as far as the length of my chain would suffer; and discharged my body of that uneasy load. But, this was the only time I was ever guilty of so uncleanly an action; for which I cannot but hope the candid reader will give some allowance, after he hath maturely and impartially considered my case, and the distress I was in. From this time my constant practice was, as soon as I rose, to perform that business in open air, at the full extent of my chain; and due care was taken every morning before company came, that the offensive matter should be carried off in wheel-barrows, by two servants appointed for that purpose. I would not have dwelt so long upon a circumstance, that perhaps at first sight may appear not very momentous; if I had not thought it necessary to justify my character in point of cleanliness to the world; which I am told, some of my maligners have been pleased, upon this and other occasions, to call in question.

When this adventure was at an end, I came back out of my house, having occasion for fresh air. The emperor was already descended from the tower, and advancing on horseback towards me, which had like to have cost him dear; for the beast, although very well trained, yet wholly unused to such a sight, which appeared, as if a mountain moved before him, reared up on his hinder feet: but that prince, who is an excellent horseman, kept his seat, until his attendants ran in, and held the bridle, while his Majesty had time to dismount. When he alighted, he surveyed me round with great admiration, but kept beyond the length of my chains. He ordered his cooks and butlers, who were already prepared, to give me victuals and drink, which they pushed forward in a sort of vehicles upon wheels until I could reach them. I took these vehicles, and soon emptied them all; twenty of them were filled with meat, and ten with liquor; each of the former afforded me two or three good mouthfuls, and I emptied the liquor of ten vessels, which was contained in earthen vials, into one vehicle, drinking it off at a draught; and so I did with the rest. The empress, and young princes of the blood, of both sexes, attended by many ladies, sate at some distance in their chairs; but upon the accident that happened to the emperor's horse, they alighted, and came near his person; which I am now going to describe. He is taller by almost the breadth of my nail, than any of his court; which alone 19 is enough to strike an awe into the beholders. His features are strong and masculine, with an Austrian lip, and arched nose, his complexion olive, his countenance erect, his body and limbs well proportioned, all his motions graceful, and his deportment majestick. He was then past his prime, being twenty-eight years and three quarters old, of which he had reigned about seven, in great felicity, and generally victorious. For the better convenience of beholding him, I lay on my side, so that my face was parallel to his, and he stood but three yards off: however, I have had him since many times in my hand, and therefore cannot be deceived in the description. His dress was very plain and simple, the fashion of it between the Asiatick and the European; but he had on his head a light helmet of gold, adorned with jewels, and a plume on the crest. He held his sword drawn in his hand, to defend himself, if I should happen to break loose; it was almost three inches long, the hilt and scabbard were gold enriched with diamonds. His voice was shrill but very clear and articulate, and I could distinctly hear it when I stood up. The ladies and courtiers were all most magnificently clad, so that the spot they stood upon seemed to resemble a petticoat spread on the ground, embroidered with figures of gold and silver.

His Imperial Majesty spoke often to me, and I returned

answers, but neither of us could understand a syllable. There were several of his priests and lawyers present (as I conjectured by their habits) who were commanded to address themselves to me, and I spoke to them in as many languages as I had the least smattering of, which were High and Low-Dutch, Latin, French, Spanish, Italian, and lingua franca; but all to no purpose. After about two hours the court retired, and I was left with a strong guard, to prevent the impertinence, and probably the malice of the rabble, who were very impatient to croud about me as near as they durst; and some of them had the imprudence to shoot their arrows at me as I sate on the ground by the door of my house; whereof one very narrowly missed my left eye. But the colonel ordered six of the ringleaders to be seized, and thought no punishment so proper as to deliver them bound into my hands, which some of his soldiers accordingly did, pushing them forwards with the but-ends of their pikes into my reach: I took them all in my right hand, put five of them into my coat-pocket; and as to the sixth, I made a countenance as if I would eat him alive. The poor man squalled terribly, and the colonel and his officers were in much pain, especially when they saw me take out my penknife: but I soon put them out of fear; for, looking mildly, and immediately cutting the strings he was bound with, I set him gently on the ground, and away he ran. I treated the rest in the same manner, taking them one by one out of my pocket; and I observed, both the soldiers and people were highly obliged at this mark of my clemency, which was represented very much to my advantage at court.

Towards night I got with some difficulty into my house, where I lay on the ground, and continued to do so about a fortnight; during which time the emperor gave orders to have a bed prepared for me. Six hundred beds of the common measure were brought in carriages, and worked up in my house; an hundred and fifty of their beds sown together made up the breadth and length, and these were four double, which however kept me but very indifferently from the hardness of the floor, that was of smooth stone. By the same computation they provided me with sheets, blankets, and coverlets, tolerable enough for one who had been so long enured to hardships as I.

As the news of my arrival spread through the kingdom, it brought prodigious numbers of rich, idle, and curious people to see me; so that the villages were almost emptied, and great neglect of tillage and household affairs must have ensued, if his Imperial Majesty had not provided by several proclamations and orders of State against this inconveniency. He directed that those, who had already beheld me, should return home, and not presume to come within fifty yards of my house, without licence from court; whereby the Secretaries of State got considerable fees.

In the mean time, the emperor held frequent councils to debate what course should be taken with me; and I was afterwards assured by a particular friend, a person of great quality, who was as much in the secret as any; that the court was under many difficulties concerning me. They apprehended my breaking loose; that my diet would be very expensive, and might cause a famine. Sometimes they determined to starve me, or at least to shoot me in the face and hands with poisoned arrows, which would soon dispatch me: but again they considered, that the stench of so large a carcase might produce a plague in the metropolis, and probably spread through the whole kingdom. In the midst of these consultations, several officers of the army went to the door of the great council-chamber; and two of them being admitted, gave an account of my behaviour to the six criminals above-mentioned; which made so favourable an impression in the breast of his Majesty, and the whole board, in my behalf, that an imperial commission was issued out, obliging all the villages nine hundred yards round the city, to deliver in every morning six beeves, forty sheep, and other victuals for my sustenance; together with a proportionable quantity of bread and wine, and other liquors: for the due payment of which his Majesty gave assignments upon his treasury. For this prince lives chiefly upon his own demesnes; seldom, except upon great occasions raising any subsidies upon his subjects, who are bound to attend him in his wars at their own expence. An establishment was also made of six hundred persons to be my domesticks, who had board-wages allowed for their maintenance, and tents built for them very conveniently on each side of my door. It was likewise ordered, that three hundred taylors should make me a suit of cloaths after the fashion of the country: that, six of his Majesty's greatest scholars should be employed to instruct me in their language: and lastly, that the emperor's horses; and those of the nobility, and troops of guards, should be exercised in my sight, to accustom themselves to me. All these orders were duly put in execution; and in about three weeks I made a great progress in learning their language; during which time, the emperor frequently honoured me with his visits, and was pleased to assist my masters in teaching me. We began already to converse together in some sort; and the first words I learnt, were to express my desire, that he would please to give me my liberty; which I every day repeated on my knees. His answer, as I could apprehend, was, that this must be a work of time, not to be thought on without the advice of his council; and that first I must 'Lumus kelmin pesso desmar lon emposo'; that is, 'Swear a peace with him and his kingdom.' However, that I should be used with all kindness; and he advised me to acquire by my patience and discreet behaviour, the good opinion of himself and his subjects. He desired I would not take it ill, if he gave orders to certain proper officers to search me; for probably I might carry about me several weapons, which must needs be dangerous things, if they answered the bulk of so prodigious a person. I said, his Majesty should be satisfied, for I was ready to strip my self, and turn up my pockets before him. This I delivered, part in words, and part in signs. He replied, that by the laws of the kingdom, I must be searched by two of his officers: that he knew this could not be done without my consent and assistance: that he had so good an opinion of my generosity and justice, as to trust their persons in my hands: that whatever they took from me should be returned when I left the country, or paid for at the rate which I would set upon them. I took up the two officers in my hands, put them first into my coat-pockets, and then into every other pocket about me, except my two fobs, and another secret pocket which I had no mind should be searched, wherein I had some little necessaries of no consequence to any but my self. In one of my fobs there was a silver watch, and in the other a small quantity of gold in a purse. These gentlemen, having pen, ink, and paper about them, made an exact inventory of every thing they saw; and when they had done, desired I would set them down, that they might deliver it to the emperor. This inventory I afterwards translated into English, and is word for word as follows.

'Imprimis, in the right coat-pocket of the great Man Mountain (for so I interpret the words "Quinbus Flestrin") after the strictest search, we found only one great piece of coarse cloth, large enough to be a foot-cloth for your Majesty's chief room of State. In the left pocket, we saw a huge silver chest, with a cover of the same metal, which we, the searchers, were not able to lift. We desired it should be opened; and one of us stepping into it, found himself up to the mid-leg in a sort of dust, some part whereof flying up to our faces, set us both a sneezing for several times together. In his right waistcoat-pocket, we found a prodigious bundle of white thin substances, folded one over another, about the bigness of three men, tied with a strong cable, and marked with black figures; which we humbly conceive to be writings; every letter almost half as large as the palm of our hands. In the left there was a sort of engine, from the back of which were extended twenty long poles, resembling the pallisado's before your Majesty's court; wherewith we conjecture the Man Mountain combs his head; for we did not always trouble him with questions, because we found it a great difficulty to make him understand us. In the large pocket on the right side of his middle cover, (so I translate the word "ransu-lo," by which they meant my breeches) we saw a hollow pillar of iron, about the length of a man, fastened to a strong piece of timber, larger than the pillar; and upon one side of the pillar were huge pieces of iron sticking out, cut into strange figures; which we know not what to make of. In the left pocket, another engine of the same kind. In the smaller pocket on the right side, were several round flat pieces of white and red metal, of different bulk: some of the white, which seemed to be silver, were so large and heavy, that my comrade and I could hardly lift them. In the left pocket were two black pillars irregularly shaped; we could not, without difficulty, reach the top of them as we stood at the bottom of his pocket: one of them was covered, and seemed all of a piece; but at the upper end of the other, there appeared a white round substance, about twice the bigness of our heads. Within each of these was inclosed a prodigious plate of steel; which, by our orders we obliged him to shew us, because we apprehended they might be dangerous engines. He took them out of their cases, and told us, that in his own country his practice was to shave his beard with one of these, and to cut his meat with the other. There were two pockets which we could not enter: these he called his fobs; they were two large slits cut into the top of his middle cover, but squeezed close by the pressure of his belly. Out of the right fob hung a great silver chain, with a wonderful kind of engine at the bottom. We directed him to draw out whatever was at the end of that chain; which appeared to be a globe, half silver, and half of some transparent metal: for on the transparent side we saw certain strange figures circularly drawn, and thought we could touch them, until we found our fingers stopped with that lucid substance. He put this engine to our ears, which made an incessant noise like that of a water-mill: and we conjecture it is either some unknown animal, or the god that he worships: but we are more inclined to the latter opinion, because he assured us, (if we understood him right, for he expressed himself very imperfectly) that he seldom did any thing without consulting it. He called it his oracle, and said it pointed out the time for every action of his life. From the left fob he took out a net almost large enough for a fisherman, but contrived to open and shut like a purse, and served him for the same use: we found therein several massy pieces of yellow metal, which if they be of real gold, must be of immense value.

'Having thus, in obedience to your Majesty's commands, diligently searched all his pockets, we observed a girdle about his waist made of the hyde of some prodigious animal; from which, on the left side, hung a sword of the length of five men; and on the right, a bag or pouch divided into two cells; each cell capable of holding three of your Majesty's subjects. In one of these cells were several globes or balls of a most ponderous metal, about the bigness of our heads, and required a strong hand to lift them: the other cell contained a heap of certain black grains, but of no great bulk or weight, for we could hold above fifty of them in the palms of our hands.

'This is an exact inventory of what we found about the body of the Man Mountain; who used us with great civility, and due respect to your Majesty's commission. Signed and sealed on the fourth day of the eighty ninth moon of your Majesty's auspicious reign.

'Clefren Frelock, Marsi Frelock.'

When this inventory was read over to the emperor, he directed me to deliver up the several particulars. He first called for my scymiter, which I took out, scabbard and all. In the mean time he ordered three thousand of his choicest troops, who then attended him, to surround me at a distance, with their bows and arrows just ready to discharge: but I did not observe it; for mine eyes were wholly fixed upon his Majesty. He then desired me to draw my scymiter, which, although it had got some rust by the sea water, was in most parts exceeding bright. I did so, and immediately all the troops gave a shout between terror and surprise; for the sun shone clear, and the reflection dazzled their eyes, as I waved the scymiter to and fro in my hand. His Majesty, who is a most magnanimous prince, was less daunted than I could expect; he ordered me to return it into the scabbard, and cast it on the ground as gently as I could, about six foot from the end of my chain. The next thing he demanded was one of the hollow iron pillars, by which he meant my pocket-pistols. I drew it out, and at his desire, as well as I could, expressed to him the use of it, and charging it only with powder, which by the closeness of my pouch, happened to escape wetting in the sea, (an inconvenience that all prudent mariners take special care to provide against) I first cautioned the emperor not to be afraid; and then I let it off in the air. The astonishment here was much greater than at the sight of my scymiter. Hundreds fell down as if they had been struck dead; and even the emperor, although he stood his ground, could not recover himself in some time. I delivered up both my pistols in the same manner as I had done my scymiter, and then my pouch of powder and bullets; begging him, that the former might be kept from fire; for it would kindle with the smallest spark, and blow up his imperial palace into the air. I likewise delivered up my watch, which the emperor was very curious to see; and commanded two of his tallest yeomen of the guards to bear it on a pole upon their shoulders, as dray-men in England do a barrel of ale. He was amazed at the continual noise it made, and the motion of the minute hand, which he could easily discern; for their sight is much more acute than ours: he asked the opinions of his learned men about him, which were various and remote, as the reader may well imagine without my repeating; although, indeed, I could not very perfectly understand them. I then gave up my silver and copper money, my purse with nine large pieces of gold, and some smaller ones; my knife and razor, my comb and silver snuff-box, my handkerchief and journal book. My scymiter, pistols and pouch, were conveyed in carriages to his

Majesty's stores; but the rest of my goods were returned me.

I had, as I before observed, one private pocket which escaped their search, wherein there was a pair of spectacles (which I sometimes use for the weakness of mine eyes), a pocket perspective, and several other little conveniencies; which being of no consequence to the emperor, I did not think my self bound in honour to discover; and I apprehended they might be lost or spoiled if I ventured them out of my possession.

CHAPTER III

The author diverts the emperor and his nobility of both sexes, in a very uncommon manner. The diversions of the court of Lilliput described. The author hath his liberty granted him upon certain conditions.

My gentleness and good behaviour had gained so far on the emperor and his court, and indeed upon the army and people in general, that I began to conceive hopes of getting my liberty in a short time. I took all possible methods to cultivate this favourable disposition. The natives came by degrees to be less apprehensive of any danger from me. I would sometimes lie down, and let five or six of them dance on my hand. And at last the boys and girls would venture to come and play at hide and seek in my hair. I had now made a good progress in understanding and speaking their language. The emperor had a mind one day to entertain me with several of the country shows; wherein they exceed all nations I have known, both for dexterity and magnificence. I was diverted with none so much as that of the rope-dancers, performed upon a slender white thread, extended about two foot, and twelve inches from the ground. Upon which, I shall desire liberty, with the reader's patience, to enlarge a little.

This diversion is only practised by those persons, who are candidates for great employments, and high favour, at court. They are trained in this art from their youth, and are not always of noble birth, or liberal education. When a great office is vacant, either by death or disgrace, (which often happens) five or six of those candidates petition the emperor to entertain his Majesty and the court with a dance on the rope; and whoever jumps the highest without falling, succeeds in the office. Very often the chief ministers themselves are commanded to shew their skill, and to convince the emperor that they have not lost their faculty. Flimnap, the Treasurer, is allowed to cut a caper on the strait rope, at least an inch higher than any other lord in the whole empire. I have seen him do the summerset several times together, upon a trencher fixed on the rope, which is no thicker than a common packthread in England. My friend Reldresal, principal Secretary for Private Affairs, is, in my opinion, if I am not partial, the second after the Treasurer; the rest of the great officers are much upon a par.

These diversions are often attended with fatal accidents, whereof great numbers are on record. I my self have seen two or three candidates break a limb. But the danger is much greater, when the ministers themselves are commanded to shew their dexterity: for, by contending to excel themselves and their fellows, they strain so far, that there is hardly one of them who hath not received a fall; and some of them two or three. I was assured, that a year or two before my arrival, Flimnap would have infallibly broke his neck, if one of the king's cushions, that accidentally lay on the ground, had not weakned the force of his fall.

There is likewise another diversion, which is only shewn before the emperor and empress, and first minister, upon particular occasions. The emperor lays on a table three fine silken threads, of six inches long. one is blue, the other red, and the third green. These threads are proposed as prizes, for those persons whom the emperor hath a mind to distinguish by a peculiar mark of his favour. The ceremony is performed in his Majesty's great chamber of State; where the candidates are to undergo a tryal of dexterity very different from the former, and such as I have not observed the least resemblance of in any other country of the Old or the New World. The emperor holds a stick in his hands, both ends parallel to the horrison, while the candidates advancing one by one, sometimes leap over the stick, sometimes creep under it backwards and forwards several times, according as the stick is advanced or depressed. Sometimes the emperor holds one end of the stick, and his first minister the other; sometimes the minister hath it entirely to himself. Whoever performs his part with most agility, and holds out the longest in leaping and creeping, is rewarded with the blue-coloured silk; the red is given to the next, and the green to the third, which they all wear girt twice round about the middle; and you see few great persons about this court, who are not adorned with one of these girdles.

The horses of the army, and those of the royal stables, having been daily led before me, were no longer shy, but would come up to my very feet, without starting. The riders would leap them over my hand as I held it on the ground; and one of the emperor's huntsmen, upon a large courser, took my foot, shoe and all; which was indeed a prodigious leap. I had the good fortune to divert the emperor one day, after a very extraordinary manner. I desired he would order several sticks of two foot high, and the thickness of an ordinary cane, to be brought me; whereupon his Majesty commanded the master of his woods to give directions accordingly; and the next morning, six wood-men arrived with as many carriages, drawn by eight horses to each. I took nine of these sticks, and fixing them firmly in the ground in a quadrangular figure, two foot and a half square; I took four other sticks, and tyed them parallel at each corner, about two foot from the ground; then I fastned my handkerchief to the nine sticks that stood erected; and extended it on all sides, until it was as tight as the top of a drum; and the four parallel sticks rising about five inches higher than the handkerchief, served as ledges on each side. When I had finished my work, I desired the emperor to let a troop of his best horse, twenty four in number, come and exercise upon this plain. His Majesty approved of the proposal, and I took them up one by one in my hands, ready mounted and armed, with the proper officers to exercise them. As soon as they got into order, they divided into two 36 parties, performed mock skirmishes, discharged blunt arrows, drew their swords, fled and pursued, attacked and retired; and in short discovered the best military discipline I ever beheld. The parallel sticks secured them and their horses from falling over the stage; and the emperor was so much delighted, that he ordered this entertainment to be repeated several days; and once was pleased to be lifted up, and give the word of command; and, with great difficulty, persuaded even the empress her self to let me hold her in her close chair, within two yards of the stage, from whence she was able to take a full view of the whole performance. It was my good fortune that no ill accident happened in these entertainments; only once a fiery horse that belonged to one of the captains, pawing with his hoof struck a hole in my handkerchief, and his foot slipping, he overthrew his rider and himself; but I immediately relieved them both: for, covering the hole with one hand, I set down the troop with the other, in the same manner as I took them up. The horse that fell was strained in the left shoulder, but the rider got no hurt; and I repaired my handkerchief as well as I could: however, I would not trust to the strength of it any more in such dangerous enterprises.

About two or three days before I was set at liberty, as I was entertaining the court with these kinds of feats, there arrived an express to inform his Majesty, that some of his subjects riding near the place where I was first taken up, had seen a great black substance lying on the ground, very oddly shaped, extending its edges round as wide as his Majesty's bed-chamber, and rising up in the middle as high as a man: that it was no living creature, as they at first apprehended; for it lay on the grass without motion, and some of them had walked round it several times: that by mounting upon each others shoulders, they had got to the top, which was flat and even; and, stamping upon it, they found it was hollow within: that they humbly conceived it might be something belonging to the Man-Mountain; and if his Majesty pleased, they would undertake to bring it with only five horses. I presently knew what they meant; and was glad at heart to receive this intelligence. It seems, upon my first reaching the shore, after our shipwreck, I was in such confusion, that before I came to the place where I went to sleep, my hat, which I had fastened with a string to my head while I was rowing, and had stuck on all the time I was swimming, fell off after I came to land; the string, as I conjecture, breaking by some accident which I never observed, but thought my hat had been lost at sea. I intreated his Imperial Majesty to give orders it might be brought to me as soon as

possible, describing to him the use and the nature of

t: and the next day the waggoners arrived with it, but not in a very good condition; they had bored two holes in the brim, within an inch and a half of the edge, and fastened two hooks in the holes; these hooks were tied by a long cord to the harness, and thus my hat was dragged along for above half an English mile: but the ground in that country being extremely smooth and level, it received less damage than I expected.

Two days after this adventure, the emperor having ordered that part of his army, which quarters in and about his metropolis, to be in a readiness, took a fancy of diverting himself in a very singular manner. He desired I would stand like a Colossus, with my legs as far asunder as I conveniently could. He then commanded his general (who was an old experienced leader, and a great patron of mine) to draw up the troops in close order, and march them under me; the foot by twenty-four in a breast, and the horse by sixteen, with drums beating, colours flying, and pikes advanced. This body consisted of three thousand foot, and a thousand horse. His Majesty gave orders, upon pain of death, that every soldier in his march should observe the strictest decency, with regard to my person; which, however, could not prevent some of the younger officers from turning up their eyes as they passed under me. And, to confess the truth, my breeches were at that time in so ill a condition, that they afforded some opportunities for laughter and admiration.

I had sent so many memorials and petitions for my liberty, that his Majesty at length mentioned the matter first in the Cabinet, and then in a full council; where it was opposed by none, except Skyresh Bolgolam, who was pleased, without any provocation, to be my mortal enemy. But it was carried against him by the whole board, and confirmed by the emperor. That minister was Galbet, or Admiral of the Realm; very much in his master's confidence, and a person well versed in affairs, but of a morose and sour complection. However, he was at length persuaded to comply; but prevailed that the articles and conditions upon which I should be set free, and to which I must swear, should be drawn up by himself. These articles were brought to me by Skyresh Bolgolam in person, attended by two under secretaries, and several persons of distinction. After they were read, I was demanded to swear to the performance of them; first in the manner of my own country, and afterwards in the method prescribed by their laws; which was to hold my right foot in my left hand, to place the middle finger of my right hand on the crown of my head, and my thumb on the tip of my right ear. But, because the reader may perhaps be curious to have some idea of the style and manner of expression peculiar to that people, as well as to know the articles upon which I recovered my liberty; I have made a translation of the whole instrument, word for word, as near as I was able; which I here offer to the publick.

'Golbasto Momaren Evlame Gurdilo Shefin Mully Ully Gue, most mighty emperor of Lilliput, delight and terror of the universe, whose dominions extend five thousand *blustrugs*, (about twelve miles in circumference) to the extremities of the globe: monarch of all monarchs: taller than the sons of men; whose feet press down to the center, and whose head strikes against the sun: at whose nod the princes of the earth shake their knees; pleasant as the spring, comfortable as the summer, fruitful as autumn, dreadful as winter. His most sublime Majesty proposeth to the Man Mountain, lately arrived at our celestial dominions, the following articles, which by a solemn oath he shall be obliged to perform.

'First, the Man Mountain shall not depart from our dominions, without our licence under our great seal.

'Secondly, he shall not presume to come into our metropolis, without our express order; at which time, the inhabitants shall have two hours warning to keep within their doors.

'Thirdly, the said Man Mountain shall confine his walks to our principal high roads; and not offer to walk or lie down in a meadow, or field of corn.

'Fourthly, as he walks the said roads, he shall take the utmost care not to trample upon the bodies of any of our loving subjects, their horses, or carriages; nor take any of our said subjects into his hands, without their own consent.

'Fifthly, if an express require extraordinary dispatch; the Man Mountain shall be obliged to carry in his pocket the messenger and horse, a six days journey once in every moon, and return the said messenger back (if so required) safe to our imperial presence.

'Sixthly, he shall be our ally against our enemies in the island of Blefuscu, and do his utmost to destroy their fleet, which is now preparing to invade us.

'Seventhly, that the said Man Mountain shall, at his times of leisure, be aiding and assisting to our workmen, in helping to raise certain great stones, towards covering the wall of the principal park, and other our royal buildings.

'Eighthly, that the said Man Mountain shall, in two
moons time, deliver in an exact survey of the

circumference of our dominions, by a computation of his own paces round the coast.

'Lastly, that upon his solemn oath to observe all the above articles, the said Man Mountain shall have a daily allowance of meat and drink, sufficient for the support of 1724 of our subjects; with free access to our royal person, and other marks of our favour. Given at our palace at Belfaborac the twelfth day of the ninty-first moon of our reign.'

I swore and subscribed to these articles with great chearfulness and content, although some of them were not so honourable as I could have wished; which proceeded wholly from the malice of Skyresh Bolgolam the High Admiral: whereupon my chains were immediately unlocked, and I was at full liberty: the emperor himself, in person, did me the honour to be by at the whole ceremony. I made my acknowledgements, by prostrating my self at his Majesty's feet: but he commanded me to rise; and after many gracious expressions, which, to avoid the censure of vanity, I shall not repeat; he added, that he hoped I should prove a useful servant, and well deserve all the favours he had already conferred upon me, or might do for the future.

The reader may please to observe, that in the last article for the recovery of my liberty, the emperor stipulates to allow me a quantity of meat and drink, sufficient for the support of 1724 Lilliputians. Some time after, asking a friend at court how they came to fix on that determinate number; he told me, that his Majesty's mathematicians, having taken the height of my body by the help of a quadrant, and finding it to exceed theirs in the proportion of twelve to one, they concluded from the similarity of their bodies, that mine must contain at least 1724 of theirs, and consequently would require as much food as was necessary to support that number of Lilliputians. By which, the reader may conceive an idea of the ingenuity of that people, as well as the prudent and exact ceconomy of so great a prince.

CHAPTER IV

Mildendo, the metropolis of Lilliput described, together with the emperor's palace. A conversation between the author and a principal secretary, concerning the affairs of that empire: the author's offers to serve the emperor in his wars.

The first request I made after I had obtained my liberty, was, that I might have licence to see Mildendo, the metropolis; which the emperor easily granted me, but with a special charge to do no hurt, either to the inhabitants, or their houses. The people had notice by proclamation of my design to visit the town. The wall which encompassed it, is two feet and an half high, and at least eleven inches broad, so that a coach and horses may be driven very safely round it; and it is flanked with strong towers at ten feet distance. I stept over the great western gate, and passed very gently, and sideling through the two principal streets, only in my short waistcoat, for fear of damaging the roofs and eves of the houses with the skirts of my coat. I walked with the utmost circumspection, to avoid treading on any stragglers, who might remain in the streets, although the orders were very strict, that all people should keep in their houses, at their own peril. The garret windows, and tops of houses were so crowded with spectators, that I thought in all my travels I had not seen a more populous place. The city is an exact square, each side of the wall being five hundred foot long. The two great streets which run cross and divided it into four quarters, are five foot wide. The lanes and alleys which I could not enter, but only viewed them as I passed, are from twelve to eighteen inches. The town is capable of holding five hundred thousand souls. The houses are from three to five stories. The shops and markets well provided.

The emperor's palace is in the center of the city, where the two great streets meet. It is inclosed by a wall of two foot high, and twenty foot distant from the buildings. I had his Majesty's permission to step over this wall; and the space being so wide between that and the palace, I could easily view it on every side. The outward court is a square of forty foot, and includes two other courts: in the inmost are the royal apartments, which I was very desirous to see, but found it extremely difficult; for the great gates, from one square into another, were but eighteen inches high, and seven inches wide. Now the buildings of the outer court were at least five foot high; and it was impossible for me to stride over them, without infinite damage to the pile, although the walls were strongly built of hewen stone, and four inches thick. At the same time, the emperor had a great desire that I should see the magnificence of his palace: but this I was not able to do until three days after, which I spent in cutting down with my knife some of the largest trees in the royal park, about an hundred yards distant from the city. Of these trees I made two stools, each about three foot high, and strong enough to bear my weight. The people having received notice a second time, I went again through the city to the palace, with my two stools in my hands. When I came to the side of the outer court, I stood upon one stool, and took the other in my hand: this I lifted over the roof, and gently set it down on the space between the first and second court, which was eight foot wide. I then stept over the buildings very conveniently from one stool to the other, and drew up the first after me with a hooked stick. By this contrivance I got into the inmost court; and lying down upon my side, I applied my face to the windows of the middle stories, which were left open on purpose, and discovered the most splendid apartments that can be imagined. There I saw the empress, and the young princes in their several lodgings, with their chief attendants about them. Her Imperial Majesty was pleased to smile very graciously upon me, and gave me out of the window her hand to kiss.

But I shall not anticipate the reader with farther descriptions of this kind, because I reserve them for a greater work, which is now almost ready for the press; containing a general description of this empire, from its first erection, through a long series of princes, with a particular account of their wars and politicks, laws, learning, and religion; their plants and animals, their peculiar manners and customs, with other matters very curious and useful; my chief design at present being only to relate such events and transactions as happened to the publick, or, to my self, during a residence of about nine months in that empire.

One morning, about a fortnight after I had obtained my liberty; Reldresal, Principal Secretary (as they stile him) of Private Affairs, came to my house, attended only by one servant. He ordered his coach to wait at a distance, and desired I would give him an hour's audience; which I readily consented to, on account of his quality, and personal merits, as well as of the many good offices he had done me during my sollicitations at court. I offered to lie down, that he might the more conveniently reach my ear; but he chose rather to let me hold him in my hand during our conversation. He began with compliments on my liberty; said, he might pretend to some merit in it; but, however, added, that if it had not been for the present situation of things at court, perhaps I might not have obtained it so soon. For, said he, as flourishing a condition as we appear to be in to foreigners, we labour under two mighty evils; a violent faction at home, and the danger of an invasion by a most potent enemy from abroad. As to the first, you are to understand, that for above seventy moons past, there have been two struggling parties in this empire, under the names of Tramecksan, and

Slamecksan, from the high and low heels on their shoes, by which they distinguish themselves.

It is alledged indeed, that the high heels are most agreeable to our ancient constitution: but however this be, his Majesty hath determined to make use of only low heels in the administration of the Government, and all offices in the gift of the Crown; as you cannot but observe; and particularly, that his Majesty's imperial heels are lower at least by a *drurr* than any of his court; (*drurr* is a measure about the fourteenth part of an inch.) The animosities between these two parties run so high, that they will neither eat nor drink, nor talk with each other. We compute the Tramecksan, or high-heels, to exceed us in number; but the power is wholly on our side. We apprehend his Imperial Highness, the heir to the crown, to have some tendency towards the high-heels; at least we can plainly discover one of his heels higher than the other; which gives him a hobble in his gait. Now, in the midst of these intestine disquiets, we are threatened with an invasion from the island of Blefuscu, which is the other great empire of the universe, almost as large and powerful as this of his Majesty. For as to what we have heard you affirm, that there are other kingdoms and states in the world, inhabited by human creatures as large as your self, our philosophers are in much doubt; and would rather conjecture, that you dropt from the moon, or one of the stars; because it is certain, that an hundred mortals of your bulk, would, in a short time, destroy all the fruits and cattle of his Majesty's dominions. Besides, our histories of six thousand moons make no mention of any other regions, than the two great empires of Lilliput and Blefuscu. Which two mighty powers have, as I was going to tell you, been engaged in a most obstinate war for six and thirty moons past. It began upon the following occasion. It is allowed on all hands, that the primitive way of breaking eggs before we eat them, was upon the larger end: but his present Majesty's grand-father, while he was a boy, going to eat an egg, and breaking it according to the ancient practice, happened to cut one of his fingers. Whereupon the emperor his father, published an edict, commanding all his subjects, upon great penalties, to break the smaller end of their eggs. The people so highly resented this law, that our histories tell us, there have been six rebellions raised on that account; wherein one emperor lost his life, and another his crown. These civil commotions were constantly fomented by the monarchs of Blefuscu; and when they were quelled, the exiles always fled for refuge to that empire. It is computed, that eleven thousand persons have, at several times, suffered death, rather than submit to break their eggs at the smaller end. Many hundred large volumes have been published upon this controversy: but the books of the Big-Endians have been long forbidden, and the whole party rendered incapable by law of holding employments. During the course of these troubles, the emperors of Blefuscu did frequently expostulate by their ambassadors, accusing us of making a schism in religion, by offending against a fundamental doctrine of our great prophet Lustrog, in the fifty-fourth chapter of the *Brundrecal*, (which is their *Alcoran*.) This, however, is thought to be a meer strain upon the text: for the words are these; 'That all true believers shall break their eggs at the convenient end': and which is the convenient end, seems in my humble opinion, to be left to every man's conscience, or at least in the power of the chief magistrate to determine. Now the Big-Endian exiles have found so much credit in the Emperor of Blefuscu's court; and so much private assistance and encouragement from their party here at home, that a bloody war hath been carried on between the two empires for six and thirty moons with various success; during which time we have lost forty capital ships, and a much greater number of smaller vessels, together with thirty thousand of our best seamen and soldiers; and the damage received by the enemy is reckoned to be somewhat greater than ours. However, they have now equipped a numerous fleet, and are just preparing to make a descent upon us: and his Imperial Majesty, placing great confidence in your valour and strength, hath commanded me to lay this account of his affairs before you.

I desired the secretary to present my humble duty to the emperor, and to let him know, that I thought it would not become me, who was a foreigner, to interfere with parties; but I was ready, with the hazard of my life, to defend his person and state against all invaders.

CHAPTER V

The author by an extraordinary stratagem prevents an invasion. A high title of honour is conferred upon him. Ambassadors arrive from the Emperor of Blefuscu, and sue for peace. The empress's apartment on fire by an accident; the author instrumental in saving the rest of the palace.

The empire of Blefuscu, is an island situated to the north north-east side of Lilliput, from whence it is
parted only by a channel of eight hundred yards wide.

I had not yet seen it, and upon this notice of an intended invasion, I avoided appearing on that side of the coast, for fear of being discovered by some of the enemies ships, who had received no intelligence of me; all intercourse between the two empires having been strictly forbidden during the war, upon pain of death; and an embargo laid by our emperor upon all vessels whatsoever. I communicated to his Majesty a project I had formed of seizing the enemies whole fleet; which, as our scouts assured us, lay at anchor in the harbour ready to sail with the first fair wind. I consulted the most experienced seamen, upon the depth of the channel, which they had often plummed; who told me, that in the middle at high water it was seventy *glumgluffs* deep, which is about six foot of European measure; and the rest of it fifty *glumgluffs* at most. I walked to the north-east coast over against Blefuscu; where, lying down behind a hillock, I took out my small pocket perspective glass, and viewed the enemy's fleet at anchor, consisting of about fifty men of war, and a great number of transports: I then came back to my house, and gave order (for which I had a warrant) for a great quantity of the strongest cable and bars of iron. The cable was about as thick as packthread, and the bars of the length and size of a knitting-needle. I trebled the cable to make it stronger; and for the same reason I twisted three of the iron bars together, binding the extremities into a hook. Having thus fixed fifty hooks to as many cables, I went back to the north-east coast, and putting off my coat, shoes, and stockings, walked into the sea in my leathern jerken, about half an hour before high water. I waded with what haste I could, and swam in the middle about thirty yards until I felt the ground; I arrived to the fleet in less than half an hour. The enemy was so frighted when they saw me, that they leaped out of their ships, and swam to shore; where there could not be fewer than thirty thousand souls. I then took my tackling, and fastning a hook to the hole at the prow of each, I tyed all the cords together at the end. While I was thus employed, the enemy discharged several thousand arrows, many of which stuck in my hands and face; and besides the excessive smart, gave me much disturbance in my work. My greatest apprehension was for mine eyes, which I should have infallibly lost, if I had not suddenly thought of an expedient. I kept, among other little necessaries, a pair of spectacles in a private pocket, which, as I observed before, had escaped the emperor's searchers. These I took out, and fastned as strongly as I could upon my nose; and thus armed went on boldly with my work in spight of the enemy's

arrows; many of which struck against the glasses of

my spectacles, but without any other effect, further than a little to discompose them. I had now fastned all the hooks, and taking the knot in my hand, began to pull; but not a ship would stir, for they were all too fast held by their anchors; so that the boldest part of my enterprize remained. I therefore let go the cord, and leaving the hooks fixed to the ships, I resolutely cut with my knife the cables that fastned the anchors; receiving about two hundred shots in my face and hands: then I took up the knotted end of the cables to which my hooks were tyed; and with great ease drew fifty of the enemy's largest men of war after me.

The Blefuscudians, who had not the least imagination of what I intended, were at first confounded with astonishment. They had seen me cut the cables, and thought my design was only to let the ships run a-drift, or fall foul on each other: but when they perceived the whole fleet moving in order, and saw me pulling at the end; they set up such a scream of grief and despair, that it is almost impossible to describe or conceive. When I had got out of danger, I stopt a while to pick out the arrows that stuck in my hands and face, and rubbed on some of the same ointment that was given me at my first arrival, as I have formerly mentioned. I then took off my spectacles, and waiting about an hour until the tyde was a little fallen, I waded through the middle with my cargo, and arrived safe at the royal port of Lilliput.

The emperor and his whole court stood on the shore, expecting the issue of this great adventure. They saw the ships move forward in a large half moon, but could not discern me, who was up to my breast in water. When I advanced to the middle of the channel, they were yet more in pain because I was under water to my neck. The emperor concluded me to be drowned, and that the enemy's fleet was approaching in a hostile manner: but he was soon eased of his fears; for the channel growing shallower every step I made, I came in a short time within hearing; and holding up the end of the cable by which the fleet was fastned, I cryed in a loud voice, 'Long live the most puissant Emperor of Lilliput!' This great prince received me at my landing with all possible encomiums, and created me a Nardac upon the spot, which is the highest title of honour among them.

His Majesty desired I would take some other opportunity of bringing all the rest of his enemy's ships into his ports. And so unmeasurable is the ambition of princes, that he seemed to think of nothing less than reducing the whole empire of Blefuscu into a province, and governing it by a viceroy; of destroying the Big-Endian exiles, and compelling that people to break the smaller end of their eggs; by which he would remain sole monarch of the whole world. But I endeavoured to divert him from this design, by many arguments drawn from the topicks of policy as well as justice: and I plainly protested, that I would never be an instrument of bringing a free and brave people into slavery: and when the matter was debated in council, the wisest part of the ministry were of my opinion.

This open bold declaration of mine, was so opposite to the schemes and politicks of his Imperial Majesty, that he could never forgive me: he mentioned it in a very artful manner at council, where, I was told, that some of the wisest appeared, at least by their silence, to be of my opinion; but others, who were my secret enemies, could not forbear some expressions, which by a side-wind reflected on me. And from this time began an intrigue between his Majesty, and a junta of ministers maliciously bent against me, which broke out in less than two months, and had like to have ended in my utter destruction. Of so little weight are the greatest services to princes, when put into the balance with a refusal to gratify their passions.

About three weeks after this exploit, there arrived a solemn embassy from Blefuscu, with humble offers of a peace; which was soon concluded upon conditions very advantageous to our emperor; wherewith I shall not trouble the reader. There were six ambassadors, with a train of about five hundred persons; and their entry was very magnificent, suitable to the grandeur of their master, and the importance of their business. When their treaty was finished, wherein I did them several good offices by the credit I now had, or at least appeared to have at court; their excellencies, who were privately told how much I had been their friend, made me a visit in form. They began with many compliments upon my valour and generosity; invited me to that kingdom in the emperor their master's name; and desired me to shew them some proofs of my prodigious strength, of which they had heard so many wonders; wherein I readily obliged them, but shall not interrupt the reader with the particulars.

When I had for some time entertained their excellencies to their infinite satisfaction and surprize, I desired they would do me the honour to present my most humble respects to the emperor their master, the renown of whose virtues had so justly filled the whole world with admiration, and whose royal person I resolved to attend before I returned to my own country. Accordingly, the next time I had the honour to see our emperor, I desired his general licence to wait on the Blefuscudian monarch, which he was

pleased to grant me, as I could plainly perceive, in a

very cold manner; but could not guess the reason, until I had a whisper from a certain person, that Flimnap and Bolgolam had represented my intercourse with those ambassadors, as a mark of disaffection, from which I am sure my heart was wholly free. And this was the first time I began to conceive some imperfect idea of courts and ministers.

It is to be observed, that these ambassadors spoke to me by an interpreter; the languages of both empires differing as much from each other as any two in Europe, and each nation priding itself upon the antiquity, beauty, and energy of their own tongues, with an avowed contempt for that of their neighbour: yet our emperor standing upon the advantage he had got by the seizure of their fleet, obliged them to deliver their credentials, and make their speech in the Lilliputian tongue. And it must be confessed, that from the great intercourse of trade and commerce between both realms; from the continual reception of exiles, which is mutual among them; and from the custom in each empire to send their young nobility and richer gentry to the other, in order to polish themselves by seeing the world, an understanding men and manners; there are few persons of distinction, or merchants, or seamen, who dwell in the maritime parts, but what can hold conversation in both tongues; as I found 59 some weeks after, when I went to pay my respects to the Emperor of Blefuscu, which in the midst of great misfortunes, through the malice of my enemies, proved a very happy adventure to me, as I shall relate in its proper place.

The reader may remember, that when I signed those articles upon which I recovered my liberty, there were some which I disliked upon account of their being too servile, neither could any thing but an extreme necessity have forced me to submit. But being now a Nardac, of the highest rank in that empire, such offices were looked upon as below my dignity; and the emperor (to do him justice) never once mentioned them to me. However, it was not long before I had an opportunity of doing his Majesty, at least, as I then thought, a most signal service. I was alarmed at midnight with the cries of many hundred people at my door; by which being suddenly awaked, I was in some kind of terror. I heard the word 'burglum' repeated incessantly; several of the emperor's court making their way through the croud, intreated me to come immediately to the Palace, where her Imperial Majesty's apartment was on fire by the carelessness of a maid of honour, who fell asleep while she was reading a romance. I got up in an instant; and orders being given to clear the way before me; and it being likewise a moon-shine night, I made a shift to get to the palace without trampling on any of the people. I found they had already applied ladders to the walls of the apartment, and were well provided with buckets, but the water was at some distance. These buckets were about the size of a large thimble, and the poor people supplied me with them as fast as they could; but the flame was so violent, that they did little good. I might easily have stifled it with my coat, which I unfortunately left behind me for haste, and came away only in my leathern jerkin. The case seemed wholly desperate and deplorable; and this magnificent palace would have infallibly been burnt down to the ground, if, by a presence of mind, unusual to me, I had not suddenly thought of an expedient. I had the evening before drank plentifully of a most delicious wine, called *glimigrim*, (the Blefuscudians call it *flunec*, but ours is esteemed the better sort) which is very diuretick. By the luckiest chance in the world, I had not discharged myself of any part of it. The heat I had contracted by coming very near the flames, and by my labouring to quench them, made the wine begin to operate by urine; which I voided in such a quantity, and applied so well to the proper places, that in three minutes the fire was wholly extinguished; and the rest of that noble pile, which had cost so many ages in erecting, preserved from destruction.

It was now day-light, and I returned to my house, without waiting to congratulate with the emperor; because although I had done a very eminent piece of service, yet I could not tell how his Majesty might resent the manner by which I had performed it: for, by the fundamental laws of the realm, it is capital in any person, of what quality soever, to make water within the precincts of the palace. But I was a little comforted by a message from his Majesty, that he would give orders to the grand justiciary for passing my pardon in form; which, however, I could not obtain. And, I was privately assured, that the empress conceiving the greatest abhorrence of what I had done, removed to the most distant side of the court, firmly resolved that those buildings should never be repaired for her use; and, in the presence of her chief confidents, could not forbear vowing revenge.